Face-off

Adapted by Alice Alfonsi

Based on the television series *Hannah Montana*, created by Michael Poryes and Rich Correll and Barry O'Brien

Part One is based on the episode written by Todd J. Greenwald

Part Two is based on the episode written by Steven Peterman and Gary Dontzig

This edition published by Parragon in 2008
Parragon
Queen Street House
4 Queen Street
Bath BA1 1HE, UK

ISBN 978-1-4075-3127-4

Printed in United Kingdom

PART ONE

Chapter One

"**W**onderful, Hannah! Brilliant!" exclaimed Liza from behind her high-priced camera. The tall, stylish woman ran one of the top photography studios in the business. And her job today was simple – capture pop-singing sensation Hannah Montana on film.

For over an hour, Miley Stewart had been trying hard to look hip, hot and Hannah-ish. Beneath her blonde wig and sunglasses, she was totally working it. But, boy, was she tired of smiling!

While Miley struck pose after pose in her glittery clothes, her dad stood a few feet away. With his big arms folded, he quietly watched the photo shoot from behind his usual disguise – a huge fake moustache, a long-haired wig and a baseball cap.

"You look gorgeous, radiant," Liza told Miley. In the background, the studio's sound system pounded out Hannah's latest hit.

"This is the life," the photographer squawked along with the song. "Hold on tight . . ."

Miley's beaming smile suddenly fell. She couldn't help it. Liza may have been a talented photographer, but she was one lousy singer.

"Stop, stop, stop!" Liza cried, seeing Miley's expression go sour. "Darling," she scolded, "we're doing an ad for skin cream, not wart removal! What *is* that face?"

Mr Stewart stepped forward. "I think it's a reaction to your *singin'*," he drawled.

Miley burst out laughing. But Liza was not amused. She narrowed her eyes on the strapping man in sunglasses. "And *you* are?" she asked pointedly.

"Hannah's manager," he replied, keeping it simple.

"Well, *Hannah's manager*," Liza rudely snapped, "I'm an award-winning photographer, so why don't you just push your tush *off* my set."

Mr Stewart frowned. Clearly, the woman needed a little more information. "I'm also her *father*," he informed her.

Liza blinked in surprise. Then she turned to her assistant. "I need a chair for Mr Montana's tush!" she shouted. "Now!"

The young man quickly brought over a chair. Mr Stewart sat.

"Comfy?" Liza asked, her voice suddenly as sweet as honey.

Mr Stewart grinned. "Like a monkey in a banana bath."

Liza pictured that idea and shuddered. "How charming." She wheeled back to face Miley. "Okay, now, Hannah darling, Magic Glow skin cream, everyone's favourite zit zapper, is using this poster to launch a worldwide campaign. So give me *jubilance* peppered with *rapture* and sprinkle it with a dash of *je ne sais quoi*."

Say *what*? Miley thought, scrunching her face up in total confusion.

"No, no, no, that's not even close," complained Liza.

Miley sighed. "Well, if you lighten up on the SAT words, it might help."

Now the photographer was the one who looked confused. Mr Stewart suppressed a chuckle and gave her a clue. "How 'bout, 'Say cheese'?"

Liza shouted over her shoulder, "I need some *cheese* for Mr Montana!"

Mr Stewart shook his head. "Slow down, there," he drawled as he moseyed over to the photographer. "All I'm saying is, you might get a little more out of Hannah if you just keep it simple."

"Yes, Mr Montana, anything you say," Liza replied through a stiff smile. Then she turned to her assistant and whispered, "Just what I need. Jethro's chicken-fried wisdom."

With a sigh, Liza looked through her viewfinder again. "Okay, Hannah . . ." she declared, "say *cheese*!"

Miley took a deep breath. She knew what the photographer wanted, but she

was so tired of posing and smiling that it wasn't easy.

Just then, she noticed her dad doing something right behind the photographer. As the Hannah Montana music played in the background, her dad began to dance – really badly.

Miley laughed. Her happy expression was genuine and beautiful. It was that million-dollar look that Liza had been waiting for.

"Perfection!" she cried, snapping away. "I've done it again!"

Chapter Two

The next morning, Miley and her friends were hanging out at Rico's, a snack shack near the beach. Behind the shack was a basketball court and Miley joined a group of kids for a game.

"You want it, try and get it," Miley challenged. She was dribbling down the court when Donny stepped in front of her.

When she couldn't get around the tall boy, he laughed in her face. "Come on," he taunted. "It's like taking candy from a baby."

Miley shook her head, looking defeated. Then she pointed to his trousers. "Your flies are down."

When Donny glanced down to check, Miley cried, "Oliver!" and passed the ball to him.

Danny spun, but Oliver was already dribbling towards the basket for a shot.

"Look out! Heads up!" Lilly cried.

Oliver was about to shoot when Lilly crashed right into him. Both of them fell to the ground.

"Come on, man, flagrant foul!" Oliver complained.

Lilly rose to her feet, looking guilty. "Sorry. My fault," she admitted.

She picked up the ball and moved to pass it back to Oliver. But she didn't seem to see him. Instead, she walked over to the basketball pole.

"Here you go," she told the pole. She held out the ball and let it go. The ball dropped to the ground.

"Nice hands, Shaq," she quipped.

Okay, thought Miley, enough is enough. She pulled her best girlfriend off the court and into the snack shack. "Lilly, why aren't you wearing your contacts?"

Lilly sighed, looking dejected. "My dog ate 'em," she admitted, "along with an entire tube of toothpaste. He's been doing *this* all morning–" Lilly licked her teeth and then stuck out her tongue.

Miley laughed. "Well, that's more toothpaste than my brother's used in his entire life."

Miley's older brother worked at Rico's and he overheard her insult.

"What a h-h-h-h-orrible thing to say," Jackson told his sister, exhaling his stinky breath all over her.

Miley held her nose and waved her hand. "Thanks for proving my point," she told him. Then she turned back to Lilly. "How are you going to sneak a peek at my poster tonight if you can't *see* it?"

Lilly shrugged. "I'll just imagine your head really big with pigeons on it."

Miley frowned and crossed her arms.

"I know you're giving me a look," said Lilly. "I just can't see it."

Miley rolled her eyes. "Don't you have glasses?"

"Oh, you mean these?" Lilly pulled out her glasses and put them on.

Miley tried to hide her shock. The glasses were huge, clunky and uglier than a hairy wart. But Lilly was her best friend and she didn't want to hurt her feelings.

"Wow . . . wee!" Miley said, stalling to

think of what to say about the dorky goggles. "Look at those . . . uh, *stylin'* specs!"

"Nice try," Lilly said flatly, then shook her head in despair. "Never let your mother buy you glasses at a place that also sells tyres."

"Hey, Truscott!" cried a tough-looking skater girl.

"Oh, no," Lilly whispered to Miley. "It's Heather."

Heather was Lilly's skateboarding rival. Both girls had been competing against each other since they'd learned to skate. Now Heather was striding across Rico's like she owned the place. As usual, her little sidekick, Kim, was trailing close behind.

Seeing the two girls coming, Lilly whipped off her glasses and hid them fast.

"Congrats on making the half-pipe

finals," Heather told Lilly with a smile. Then she grimaced. "I'm so sorry."

"About what?" Lilly asked.

"Sorry I'm going to beat you," Heather replied. "Again."

"Beat you again!" Kim repeated.

"You've got no chance," Heather declared.

"No chance!" Kim echoed.

Heather glanced at Kim. "Shut up!"

"Shut up!" Kim started to say, then realized that the last comment was meant for her. "Oh."

"You're the one who's got no chance," Lilly replied. Unfortunately, without her glasses, she went nose to nose with Kim instead of Heather.

"Okay, that's it," said Miley, standing up for her friend. "Listen, slick," she told Heather. "No one talks to my girl like that.

And Saturday night in the finals, you're going down! You may have beaten Lilly last year and the year before and the year—"

"I think she gets it!" Lilly interjected.

Heather turned to Lilly. "You're the one who's going to get it bad."

"Get it baaaaaad!" repeated little Kim. Then she noticed Heather giving her a *you're getting tiresome* look. "Too much?"

"You think?" Heather spat. Then she turned on her heel and stomped away with Kim right behind her.

"You may be the *champion* now," Miley called after her, "but after Saturday, you're going to be the *chumpion*!" She turned to Lilly. "High five."

Miley raised her hand and Lilly swung to slam it. But Lilly missed her best friend's hand and struck her forehead instead.

"Ow!" cried Miley.

Just then, Lilly's mobile phone rang.

"Please, answer your phone," said Miley, rubbing her head, "before you hurt somebody else."

Lilly pulled out her phone and answered. "Hello. Hi, Mum . . . what?! . . . but they said . . ." Lilly listened some more, but the news was obviously bad. "Okay, bye," she finally said.

Miley waited for an explanation.

"My contacts aren't coming in till next week," Lilly informed her.

"Big deal," Miley replied with a shrug. "You'll just wear your glasses to the finals. Who cares?"

"I do!" Lilly cried. "No way I'm going to compete if I have to wear these."

"Are you kidding me?" Miley exclaimed. "All you've been talking about is how you're going to double kick-flip Heather all over that skate park this year."

"That was with two eyes, not four," countered Lilly. "I'm not going in front of all those people looking like this."

Miley threw up her hands. "Will you forget about how you look? It's what's on the inside that counts."

Lilly folded her arms. "Easy for you to say. You're the poster child for perfect skin."

"This isn't about me," Miley replied. "Or my perfect skin." Just then, she spotted Oliver at the counter, buying a taco from her brother. "Hey, Oliver, would you please tell Lilly that looks don't matter?"

"Okay," he said, wandering over. "Looks don't matter."

Miley turned back to Lilly. "See? If Oliver can say that with his nostril thing, you can get over your glasses."

"Yeah," Oliver agreed. Then he froze. "What?"

"You know," Miley told Oliver, "how one is way bigger than the other."

Oliver stared at her, dumbfounded.

Miley turned back to Lilly. "But you don't see him obsessing over it."

Oliver immediately grabbed a stainless-steel serviette dispenser. He examined his reflection in the shiny surface.

"Look at me!" he howled. "I'm a lopsided freak!"

Miley frowned. "I'm sorry, I thought you knew."

Totally disturbed, Oliver headed home. As he crossed the sand dunes, he passed some sunbathers who innocently glanced his way.

Oliver didn't think it was so innocent. "Stop staring at me!" he shrieked. "I'm not an animal!"

The sunbathers just scratched their heads in confusion as Oliver raced away.

Chapter Three

That afternoon, Miley's father was unloading the dishwasher in the kitchen.

"Plate, cup, bowl," he recited to himself. "Glass, pot, underpants . . . What the–?"

He stared at the neon-coloured briefs. There was no way they were his. Or Miley's. That left only one other person.

"Jackson," Mr Stewart muttered. "There's something wrong with that boy."

Just then, the front door opened.

Mr Stewart looked up to see his teenage son trudging in.

"Why?" Jackson griped. "Why me? Why?"

"I was asking myself that *same* question not five seconds ago," Mr Stewart told him, "when I unloaded *these*."

Mr Stewart held up the underpants – stretched out across a dinner plate, no less. Jackson rushed over to check it out.

"Whoa, it worked!" he cried excitedly. "They're clean again–"

Mr Stewart slung the briefs into his son's face.

"–and lemon fresh!" Jackson happily added.

"On the bright side," said Mr Stewart, "I'm glad to see you're *wearing* underwear again."

Jackson nodded.

"So," said Mr Stewart, "how did your date go?"

"I still can't believe it. I finally got Jill to go out with me, we're cruising down the coastal road, I did that yawn thing, got my arm around her. And then . . ." Jackson made a raspberry noise.

Mr Stewart cringed. "Well, I can see how that could be embarrassing. At least you were in a convertible."

"Dad, it wasn't *me*," Jackson said. "It was the car! I didn't have enough money to fill it up and I ran out of petrol. It was *humiliating*."

"Don't sweat it, son," said Mr Stewart. "I'm sure your friend understood. It's not as if you made her get out and push."

"Well, actually . . ." Jackson began. But he was interrupted when the front door opened.

In came Jackson's date. Jill was a pretty sixteen year old, but at the moment she looked a total wreck. After pushing Jackson's car down the coastal road, she was sweaty, dirty, exhausted – and *really* unhappy.

"This has been the worst date of my entire life!" she exclaimed.

Jackson tried to look sympathetic. He walked over to her and grinned. "Maybe a little kiss will make it better?"

Jill knocked down the peak of Jackson's cap, then stomped back out of the door.

Mr Stewart couldn't believe his son had treated his date like that. He glared at the boy. But Jackson felt completely justified.

"Well, somebody had to steer," he said defensively.

* * *

The next day, Jackson was back working behind the counter at Rico's.

"Here you go, sir," he said, handing a customer his order. "Nice, cold bottle of water. And your change . . . which I'm putting right next to the conveniently located *tip jar*."

Actually, it would have been really hard for the man to miss the tip jar. There was a big, red, flashing neon sign right in front of it that read TIPS!

"And, may I say," Jackson added in a syrupy sweet voice, "that's a very handsome shirt."

But when the customer took his change and departed without leaving so much as a buffalo nickel, Jackson's sweet voice turned sour. "And about that shirt — my grandma's got a sofa just like it!"

Jackson started to consider a *bigger* neon sign for the jar, when a dark-haired kid wandered over.

"Hello . . . *Jackson*," said the kid with venom.

"Hello . . . *Rico*," Jackson replied with equal venom.

"So," Rico began, "your boss – the man I call *Daddy* – tells me you asked him for a raise?"

"Yeah, I did," Jackson replied. "Girls like cars, cars like petrol and petrol costs money. What's it to you?"

"Well, *Daddy* still hasn't made up his mind," Rico informed him. "Could go either way. If only you had someone on the *inside*. Someone who knows how to pull on his heartstrings and make him dance like a little puppet."

Jackson rolled his eyes. Rico was

obviously referring to himself. "What do you want, Rico?"

Rico's reply was a slow, sly smile.

"And now," Rico announced an hour later, "the Great Ricolini will perform the legendary disappearing egg trick!"

Rico was standing on the beach behind his father's fast-food shack. He was dressed in a black cape and top hat and holding a magic wand. A small crowd had gathered to watch his act.

"I'll just need the help of my charming assistant," he told the crowd, "the lovely Tina!"

Hearing his introduction, Jackson stepped out of the girls' bathroom. He was decked out in the costume Rico had given him – a glittery gold dress with a short skirt and long, white gloves.

I can't believe I agreed to this, Jackson thought. Apparently, Rico had been fantasizing about doing a magic act for months. All he needed was a female assistant. The only problem was – he couldn't find any females willing to help him out. Now Jackson was stuck pretending to be 'the lovely Tina'.

Carrying a velvet pillow with an egg on it, Jackson moved to stand beside Rico the Magician. As soon as he got there, Rico nudged Jackson to remind him about the speech they'd rehearsed.

"Here, oh Great Ricolini," Jackson recited flatly. "The magical egg. Please, no flash photography."

"Isn't she wonderful?" Rico declared to the crowd. Then he whispered to Jackson, "Come on, Tina, work it."

Jackson didn't move. Rico rubbed his

fingers in the universal sign for cash. And Jackson reluctantly struck a sexy pose.

Rico grinned. He took the egg from Jackson's pillow and addressed the crowd. "I hold in my hand what looks like an ordinary egg . . . But is it?"

He smashed the egg on Jackson's head. "Yes, it is!" Rico cried.

The crowd screamed with laughter and Rico bowed.

"And I thank you!" he told them.

Jackson wanted to strangle the kid. But then he pictured his car without petrol and himself without a date.

I had *better* get a raise out of this, Jackson told himself as yolk dripped down his face. Or I'll be making the Great Ricolini disappear.

Chapter Four

"Lilly, there's no one up here!" Miley cried, later that night. "This is really getting stupid."

Miley's father huffed and puffed as he carried Lilly the last few steps to the roof. "Oh, we passed *stupid* on the third floor," he grumbled. "Now we're up to *sports hernia*."

Miley was desperate to check out the big Hannah poster. And she wanted her best friend to see it, too. But Lilly had refused to wear her dorky glasses in public.

And without her glasses, she couldn't *see* the steps they had to climb. So Mr Stewart carried Lilly all the way up, piggyback style.

"Okay, fine," said Lilly. Mr Stewart put her down on the rooftop and she put on her glasses. "Wow!" she exclaimed, finally able to see. "This is cool!" Then she noticed Miley staring at her.

"What?" Lilly demanded.

"You know, those glasses really don't look that bad," she said sincerely.

"You're not just saying that?" Lilly asked with a flicker of hope. "They really look okay?"

Miley nodded. "Good enough to beat Heather at the finals."

Lilly thought it over. "Well . . ." she said.

Mr Stewart could see the girl needed more convincing. "If it helps you," he told her, "I think they're pretty cool."

Lilly's hopeful expression crumbled. "Aw, man!" she exclaimed, throwing up her hands.

Mr Stewart looked at Miley in total confusion. "What?" he asked.

"She was *this* close!" Miley whispered, holding two fingers an inch apart. "I almost had her!"

Mr Stewart still didn't follow. "What'd I say?"

Miley sighed. "Dad, when a parent says something's cool, you *know* it's dorky."

"Okay, I get it," Mr Stewart told Miley. Then he turned once more to face his daughter's best friend. "Lilly," he said sincerely, "the truth is, those glasses are a big bowl of ugly."

Lilly gasped. "Thanks a lot!"

Miley couldn't believe her dad. *Now* her

best friend was near tears. She turned to her clueless father and cried, "Why don't you just push her off the roof?!"

Mr Stewart massaged his temples. The pain in his back was nothing compared to this! "You girls sure were easier when you were eight," he griped. "I'd say, 'That's a pretty dress,' and you'd say, 'Thank you, Mr Stewart'."

Miley rolled her eyes and Mr Stewart clapped his hands and declared, "Okay, enough chitchat. Let's have a look at this thing."

He walked to the side of the big poster. A sheet still covered it and he began to yank it off.

Miley turned her back on the poster. She was still worried about her bestie. "Lilly, trust me," she said, gripping her friend's shoulder. "When you beat Heather, no one's going to be looking at your glasses. They're going to be looking at that big trophy in your hand."

Lilly thought it over. "It *is* big, isn't it?"

"Oh, yeah," said Miley. "And if this were me, I wouldn't let how I *look* stop me from going after it."

"Really?" Lilly's eyes opened wide, but not because of what Miley had said. Mr Stewart had just finished uncovering the Hannah Montana poster. And Lilly couldn't believe what was sitting on her friend's twenty-foot-high face.

"What if you had a zit the size of an extra-large pizza?" Lilly asked.

Miley waved her hand. "Come on. Now you're just being ridiculous."

"Oh, yeah?" said Lilly. "Turn around."

Miley spun and saw the uncovered poster. Hannah's million-dollar smile was right there from the photo shoot. But so was something else – something that hadn't been there on the day of the shoot. A large, ugly zit had been added to her forehead. The slogan on the ad read: *Even I get zits*.

"Holy zit!" Miley cried.

Her father was also stunned. "Man," he said, "that thing's big enough to have its own chairlift!"

"Chairlift?" said Lilly. "It's big enough to have its own postcode!"

Miley folded her arms. "Why don't I just wait in the car until you've finished making fun of me?!"

"Sorry, Mile," said her dad. "Don't worry, I'm going to find out what's going on. This has to be a mistake. A big, red, blotchy–"

"That's it!" Miley cried. "I'm going to the car!"

As soon as they got home, Miley's dad called the photographer. Unfortunately, the conversation didn't go very well.

". . . No, ma'am. No way," said Mr Stewart, trying to control his anger. "We never agreed to something like this."

"I know, but I had an inspiration," Liza replied on the other end of the phone line.

The stylish woman was in the middle of a photo shoot. She wore a hands-free headset as she moved around her studio, taking pictures of her latest subject.

"What inspiration?" asked Mr Stewart.

Liza shrugged. "If Hannah Montana says, 'Even I get zits', she should *have* a zit. It was staring me right in the face."

Mr Stewart gripped the phone tighter. "Now it's staring *Los Angeles* right in the face and we don't like it."

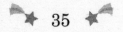

"I hear your concerns," Liza cooed, trying to smooth Mr Stewart's ruffled feathers. "Believe me, there's nothing more important to me right now than your feelings – uh, be right back!"

Liza crossed her studio and approached her photographic subject. "I need more emotion!" she told him. "You're running through a meadow! The sun is shining. You're happy. You're in love!"

For a moment, the sad old hound dog just sat there in his superhero cape, listening to Liza's direction. Then he yawned and began to howl.

Liza threw up her hands. "I can't work with this!"

While Mr Stewart waited for Liza to return to their conversation, he wandered outside to the beach-house porch.

Lilly and Miley remained in the living

room, talking. Well, *actually*, Lilly was talking. Miley was moping.

"So," said Lilly, "not so easy when it's *your* face that has a problem."

Miley knew that Lilly was right. Unless she wanted to look like a hypocrite, she had to pretend the zit was okay.

"I don't have a problem," Miley told her best friend. "Why should I have a problem? After all, looks don't matter. And if that's the way they want to go with this *worldwide* campaign, I'll be fine with it."

Just then, her dad came back inside. "Sorry, sweetheart," he said, "but that's the way they want to go with this *worldwide* campaign."

What!? Miley wanted to scream. But Lilly was staring right at her, so instead she said, "Really? Great . . . terrific . . . awesome! I love it!"

Mr Stewart scratched his head. "You do?"

"Yes, I *do*," she pointedly told her dad. Then she turned back to Lilly. "When I say, 'Looks don't matter', I mean it. Because I don't just talk the talk, I walk the walk."

Lilly's eyebrows rose. "You are amazing. I mean, if you can stand up in front of the whole world with that *ginormous* zit, something any normal person would be humiliated by–"

Miley squirmed. "Get to the point, Lilly."

"The point is," Lilly said, "if you can do all that, I can wear my glasses to that skateboarding competition."

Miley was floored. Wow, she thought. I did it. I actually convinced Lilly to wear her glasses.

"Thank you so much," Lilly said, hugging Miley tight. "This is the greatest thing you've ever done for me. I am going to double kick-flip Heather all over that skate park! Thanks to you."

Miley remained speechless as she watched her best friend head out of the door. Mr Stewart crossed over to his daughter and put an arm around her. "I'm proud of ya, Mile," he said.

But Mr Stewart might not be so proud when he found out what Miley was planning to do next.

Chapter Five

The next day didn't get any better for Jackson Stewart.

"And for my next trick," Rico announced, "the Great Ricolini will make the tempting Tina disappear!"

Jackson was back in his gold dress and white gloves. Just like the day before, Rico had attracted a small crowd near the back of his father's beach-front snack shack. Now the kid was gesturing for Jackson to squeeze into a cage.

"Tina?" Rico prompted.

Jackson stared at the little cage. He wanted a raise, but this was where he drew the line. "Ain't gonna happen," he told Rico.

Rico smiled, pulled out a twenty-dollar note and dropped it into the cage. "Fetch," he said.

Okay, thought Jackson, so I'm a dude with no shame. He climbed in after the twenty.

"Go get it, Tina," Rico taunted. "Good girl."

He shut the cage door tight and turned to the audience. "Now watch closely as I make Tina disappear!" He covered the cage with a blanket and waved his wand. "One, two . . ."

The Great Ricolini never got to *three*. Instead, he turned to two men in courier outfits. "Okay, boys!" he cried. "Take it away!"

The first courier stepped up. "Where's this going, kid?"

Rico grinned. "San Diego Zoo. And don't feed him, he bites."

"Ricooooooooo!" Jackson cried as the two couriers wheeled him away.

But Rico wasn't listening. He was too busy taking his bow. "And I thank you," he told his applauding audience.

By that night, Jackson was free again — and on a top-secret mission. He and Miley had dressed in black from head to toe. Together they climbed to the roof of the building where the Hannah Montana poster was located.

"Come on, Jackson," whispered Miley. "We've got to do this fast."

Jackson didn't move a muscle. He just stood on the rooftop, holding a paint roller and a tin of paint. "Sorry," he told his sister, "I need my cash up front. I've got one kid yanking my chain already. I don't need another."

"Fine." Miley slapped a ten-dollar note onto his waiting palm. "Half now and half when you complete the job."

"Done," said Jackson. He pocketed the cash, then removed the sheet covering the poster.

"Whoa," he said, looking at the giant zit. "I hope we brought enough paint."

Miley was about to tell him what he could do with his paint, when the roar of a helicopter interrupted her. The helicopter swooped right towards them. Its spotlight swept the area.

Miley freaked and grabbed her brother's

arm. "Do they allow makeup in prison?"

"It's just a traffic helicopter," Jackson replied. "Stay out of the light."

Miley and Jackson jumped down. They dodged the sweeping beam and hid in a shadowy corner of the rooftop.

A minute later, the helicopter's spotlight swept the poster and froze on Hannah's forehead. The pilot's voice came over the helicopter's loudspeaker.

"Bill," he said, "check out the size of that zit. I think we found the cause of the traffic jam."

Miley jumped up in outrage. "Hey!"

"Get down!" Jackson warned, pulling her back into the shadows.

After the helicopter left, Miley and Jackson moved back to the poster. Miley grabbed the paint roller and climbed onto her brother's shoulders.

"What are you going to tell Lilly at the

big unveiling when she sees the zit is gone?" Jackson asked.

"Not a problem," said Miley, working the roller. "She'll be at the skateboard competition. By the time she sees this, she'll have her trophy and I'll have my face back . . . " With a final flourish, she finished making her zit – and her problem – disappear. "Just . . . like . . . that."

"Nice work," called a deep voice.

"Thanks," Miley replied. "You know, sometimes that voice in my head sounds exactly like Dad."

"There's a reason for that," said the deep voice.

Miley and Jackson turned to see who'd just spoken. Mr Stewart put his hands on his hips.

"Nothing makes me happier than seein' my kids working together. So, who was the mastermind behind this operation?"

"Okay," said Miley with a *you-caught-me* shrug. "Jackson made me do it."

"What?" Jackson cried.

By now, brother and sister were standing beside their dad. Miley noticed a paintbrush sticking out of her father's pocket.

"Hey, Dad," she said. "Why do you have a paintbrush?"

"Okay," said Mr Stewart with his own *you-caught-me* shrug. "Jackson made me do it."

"What?!" Jackson cried.

Mr Stewart turned to his daughter. "Mile, you know I'll always be there for you. You're my little girl."

Father and daughter hugged. And Jackson folded his arms. "Hey," he said, tapping his dad's shoulder. "What am I?"

Mr Stewart shrugged. "Tina. My other

little girl."

The next morning, Jackson was back at Rico's snack shack, working hard behind the counter. The Great Ricolini strode up and dropped onto a stool.

Jackson smiled at the kid. "So, Rico," he said, "check this out." He pointed to three coconut shells sitting on the counter. He lifted one to show Rico that a red ball sat underneath.

"What's this?" Rico asked.

"Your little magic act inspired me," Jackson said. "Keep your eye on the ball." He covered up the red ball again and began to shuffle the coconuts. "It goes round and round. The amazing works of Jacksoni! Now, where's the ball?"

"Nice try, amateur," Rico scoffed. He lifted the correct coconut, revealing the red ball. "You call that a trick?"

"No," said Jackson. "I call that a *setup*. Here's the trick." Jackson reached up and pulled on a rope. A bucket, rigged above Rico, turned over and poured seaweed all over the kid's head.

Rico grimaced at the smelly, wet mess.

Ha! Jackson thought. Revenge is always so *sweet*. "You want this?" he asked, holding out a towel. "Fetch."

Jackson threw the towel across the snack shack and Rico ran after it.

"Your dad called me this morning," Jackson called after Rico. "I got the raise." With a grin, the Great Jacksoni bowed. "And I thank you."

Rico furiously gritted his teeth. "This isn't over," he promised, stomping back with the towel.

But it was over for Jackson. He started dancing around. "I got the *ra-aise*," he sang, "and dumped that *o-on* you—"

"Jackson?" a pretty girl interrupted.

It was Jill, Jackson's date from the other day – the one who'd pushed his car all the way home.

"Jill! Good news!" Jackson exclaimed. "I'm a man with money! And a lot of gas." When she gave him a funny look, he clarified. ". . . In my *car*."

"What did you do to this little boy?" Jill demanded, pointing at Rico.

"First of all," said Jackson, "he's not a little boy."

But Rico's eyes were already glimmering with an evil idea. "I want my mummy!" Rico cried.

"Stop that!" Jackson demanded.

"No, you stop," Rico whined. He stuck his thumb in his mouth and turned to Jill. "Make him stop, nice lady."

Jill patted Rico on the head. She turned and glared at Jackson. "And to think I was coming over here to give you a second chance," she scolded.

"But—" Jackson began.

Jill turned back to Rico. "It's okay," she cooed.

"He's the devil!" Jackson blurted out.

"And you're pathetic," Jill replied. Then she took Rico's hand. "Come on, sweetie, I'll take you home and wash you off."

Rico continued his fake sobs as Jill led him away. "I prefer sponge baths," he informed her as Jackson whimpered.

"But . . . but . . . I have money," Jackson called, pulling out his wallet and waving the cold, hard cash.

Unfortunately, it no longer mattered. With one last, evil smile, the Great Ricolini made Jackson's date disappear.

Chapter Six

Later that day was the official unveiling of Hannah's poster. A podium and microphone had been set up on the rooftop and a crowd had gathered to watch the famous Liza talk about her latest work.

Miley arrived with her dad. Both were wearing their Montana disguises. Miley had on her blonde Hannah wig, cool sunglasses and pop-star clothes. And her dad was dressed in his manager's outfit, complete with big moustache, long hair and baseball cap.

Together, father and daughter made their way past two large security guards, a group of press photographers and a number of important guests.

Liza was in the middle of the crowd, preening like a peacock. "Who wants to talk to me?" she loudly asked. "Oh, hi!" she said to a young local reporter, then changed her mind and shoved him away. "No, you're not important enough."

Suddenly, she spotted Miley and her father arriving. "Ah, it's the Montana posse," she said, walking over to them. "*Howdy*. And once again, I am sorry about . . . what *was* I sorry about?"

Miley's father crossed his arms. "Putting that zit on my child's forehead without our permission," he reminded her.

Liza stiffened. "Right, well . . ." She inched away, glancing around. "Who *else* wants to talk to me?"

Just then, Hannah heard a "Pssst!" She turned to see Lilly waving at her. A burly security guard had stopped her at the door and she was trying to get Hannah's attention.

Omigosh, thought Hannah. She exchanged a worried look with her father. *Why* is Lilly here?

Her father just shrugged.

Hannah faced the door again. She waved to the guard to allow Lilly inside.

"Lilly, what are you doing here?" Hannah asked when her friend bounded over. "You're *supposed* to be at the skateboard competition."

Lilly nodded. "I'm going straight from here."

She opened her long coat to show off her colourful skater gear, with matching knee and elbow pads. Her helmet was in the rucksack slung over her shoulder. And she was already wearing her big, dorky glasses.

She shrugged. "What kind of friend would I be if I didn't come to support you after all you did for me?"

Hannah gulped. "That is so sweet. Thank you so much . . . now *go*."

"No, no, no," Lilly insisted. "When they pull that cover off and expose that big zit, I'm going to be right here for you."

"Again," Hannah said. "*Appreciate* it, now *go*."

"Ladies and gentlemen," Liza announced at the podium.

Uh-oh, Hannah thought. The presentation's *starting*! And Lilly isn't *leaving*!

"I'd like to present my latest masterpiece," Liza continued. "The worldwide premiere of the Magic Glow skin cream campaign!"

Liza pulled the cord and the sheet fell away. She gestured proudly to the poster, then realized something was missing.

"Where is her zit?" Liza murmured, totally confused.

Lilly was confused, too. She stared up at Hannah's face. "Hey, what happened to the zit?" she asked Hannah. "Where'd it go?"

Hannah gulped, trying to think of an explanation. "Wow!" she finally cried. "That zit cream is *good*!"

The photographer wasn't buying it. She just kept staring at the poster. Then a thought occurred to her and she turned to glare at Mr Stewart.

"Where's my zit?" Liza loudly de-manded. "I loved that zit!"

Mr Stewart didn't flinch. "That'll teach you to sell us a horse and deliver a donkey."

That's when it hit Lilly. She wheeled on Hannah. "You covered it up!" she cried.

"Lilly," Hannah pleaded, "you don't understand."

"Oh, I understand fine," Lilly shot back. "You *lied* to me. All that stuff about 'Looks don't matter, it's what's on the inside' – you never meant a word of it."

"Yes, I did . . . until it was my face," Hannah admitted. "Look, just because I couldn't take my own advice doesn't mean you shouldn't! Go to that skateboard competition. Teach me a lesson. Be my role model."

Lilly snapped her fingers. "Save it," she told Hannah, tearing off her dorky glasses.

"Why should I believe anything you tell me?"

"Because . . ." Hannah said, thinking fast, "you said it was the best thing I ever did for you."

"Well . . ." Lilly replied, "sometimes I say things I don't mean. *You* should know what *that's* like."

Hannah couldn't believe it. Lilly was furious and now she was leaving. "Lilly–"

Hannah crossed the roof to stop Lilly, but she had to walk right past Liza at the podium. And the angry photographer wasn't about to let Hannah Montana get away clean.

"Well, here she is," Liza announced into the microphone, "the new Magic Glow skin girl . . . Miss Can't-Even-Have-One-Li'l-Blemish-No-Matter-How-Many-Awards-I'd-Win-If-She-Did."

Hannah tried to get past, but Liza

grabbed her arm. "Ladies and gentlemen," Liza cried, "Hannah Montana!"

Stuck at the podium, Hannah signalled to the security guard by the door. "Don't let her go," she demanded, pointing to Lilly.

The big guard nodded and blocked Lilly's path. Lilly was a pretty good dodge artist, but this guy was a rock. And without her glasses on, she just couldn't get past him.

Meanwhile, as Hannah moved to the microphone, the crowd applauded. "Thank you," she said. "It's a real honour to be a spokesperson for Magic Glow skin cream. And if I've learned anything from this experience, it's that nobody's perfect, even celebrities."

"You look pretty perfect up there," Lilly angrily shouted by the door.

Hannah felt terrible. This is stupid, she

thought. And it's totally not worth losing my best friend. But what can I do?

Spying a bucket of water on the podium, Hannah had an idea. She took the bucket in her hand. "Yeah, sometimes I do look pretty perfect," Hannah admitted. "But sometimes, I look like this–"

With one grand toss, she threw the water onto the poster. The water washed the paint away from the giant zit.

The photographer happily clapped her hands and the crowd began to murmur.

Curious, Lilly put her glasses back on. "Whoa," she whispered, seeing what Hannah had done.

Mr Stewart looked up at the poster, then down at his daughter – and smiled proudly.

Hannah shrugged. "I didn't want people seeing me that way," she confessed to the crowd, "but I was wrong." She met Lilly's *four* eyes. "Looks aren't everything . . . I mean, I'm not going to say they don't matter, but there's a lot of stuff that matters more. And if you let a zit or, say, *dorky glasses*, stop you from living your life, you're going to regret it. You really will."

Hannah held her breath, waiting to see what Lilly would do. She didn't have to wait long. Lilly gave her best friend a huge thumbs-up.

Hannah grinned. "So take your pictures," she told the crowd. "Let the world see that even Hannah Montana has zits." She gestured to her poster. "And I'm okay with it."

Just then, a fluttering shadow crossed Hannah's face.

PLOP!

She sighed. A bird had left its sticky

white calling card on her shoulder. *Gross*, she thought. Zits are one thing, but . . . "*This*," she admitted, "I ain't so crazy about."

Sheesh, Miley thought. I never knew life as a superstar would be so hard!

PART TWO

PART TWO

Chapter One

The lipstick came out of nowhere.

Well, actually, it came out of Amber's designer handbag. She passed it to her best friend, Ashley, who slathered it all over Oliver Oken's mouth.

Oliver never saw it coming — mainly because his eyes were closed. He had nodded off at his desk while waiting for class to start.

"Oh, yeah, baby," Oliver murmured as Ashley painted his lips a stylin' shade of bubble-gum pink.

Kids gathered around Oliver's desk and sniggered. Oliver didn't hear them. Beneath his shaggy-dog fringe, he remained happily in dreamland.

"I love you, too," he mumbled.

Ashley tossed her long, dark hair and giggled. She and Amber loved being popular. Tormenting a kid like Oliver was just their idea of a good time.

When Oliver puckered up, Ashley dug around in her new pink rucksack. Her manicured fingers closed around an orange. She put it to Oliver's lips. Still in dreamland, he kissed the fruit.

As the kids around him shrieked with laughter, Oliver woke with a start. He saw the orange, smeared with lipstick and smacked his forehead.

"Oh, man!" he cried. "Not again!"

"Meet your new girlfriend," Amber

taunted. She grabbed the orange from Ashley and waved it in front of his face.

"Hey, Oken," called a popular boy named Donny, "is she your main *squeeze*?" He turned to the crowd of kids around Oliver. "Get it, *squeeze*? *Orange*? Where do I come up with this stuff?"

As Donny high-fived his friends, two girls pushed their way through the gawking group. One of them was Miley Stewart.

Miley was a good friend of Oliver's. She was also Hannah Montana, the hottest teen pop singer around. She lived in a fabulous Malibu beach house. She had millions of fans. And she was very good at keeping her rock-star life a secret. Unfortunately, Miley *wasn't* very good at keeping Oliver out of trouble.

"Hey, leave him alone!" Miley yelled.

"Yeah," said her best friend, Lilly Truscott.

Lilly was a tomboy and a skateboarding fanatic and she wasn't afraid of anyone. In other words, she was great to have around during face-offs like this. She and Oliver were the only friends of Miley who knew about her secret Hannah Montana life.

"Nobody picks on Oliver but *us*," Lilly declared.

"That's right!" Oliver agreed. Then he realized *what* he was agreeing to. "Hey!"

Miley shook her head at the sight of his pink glossed mouth. "I mean, if we were going to pick on Oliver, we easily could've said, 'Man, you make an *ugly* girl'."

Lilly nodded. "But we didn't . . . even though it's true."

"Thanks!" said Oliver. "Hey!"

Just then, the classroom door opened,

and in came the teacher. "Okay, people," said Mr Picker, clapping his hands. "It's pop quiz time!"

The class moaned as they took their seats. And Mr Picker smiled. He *loved* the sound of students moaning in the morning!

"Who can tell me why this is the worst day of my life?" he asked.

Like a wild man, Oliver waved his hand.

In the seat behind him, Milo smacked his forehead. "Don't do it," he warned his friend. "You *never* get this right."

But Oliver was in his own little world, totally determined to answer. "I know why it's the worst day of your life, Mr Picker!" he blurted out. "You got passed over for principal again, right?"

Mr Picker frowned and narrowed his eyes. "That's right, Oken, poke the bear with a stick, why don't you? *No*, it's not that–" The teacher finally noticed Oliver's lipstick. "And by the way," Mr Picker told him, "that's not your colour."

Oliver blushed pinker than the makeup on his mouth. He wiped it off with his sleeve.

"Anyway," the teacher continued, pulling papers from his briefcase, "my *joy* today is because I lost a bet with Coach Hendricks and am now the chaperone of this year's class camping trip."

Once again, the class moaned.

"Oh, don't moan. It's going to be great," Mr Picker told them. "Sitting by the campfire, telling stories, being eaten alive by disease-ridden insects . . ." The teacher sighed and shook his head. "How did Hendricks fit an entire cantaloupe in his mouth? I saw it and I still don't believe it."

"Oh, come *on*," Miley drawled, her Southern accent coming out. "Campin's

Part One

"So," said Mr Stewart, "how did your date go?"

"Lilly, trust me," Miley said. "When you beat Heather, no one's going to be looking at your glasses."

Miley couldn't believe it when she saw the Magic Glow poster. The photographer had added an extra-large zit to her forehead!

"Whoa," said Jackson, checking out the giant
zit. "I hope we brought enough paint."

Miley and her father – Mr Stewart – arrived at the poster unveiling in their disguises.

"Take your pictures," Hannah told the crowd. "Let the world see that even Hannah Montana has zits."

Part Two

"It was the sixth day without food," Oliver declared. "Only one man could guide the remaining survivors to safety: Oliver Oscar Oken."

Lilly pulled a catapult out of her pocket. "I've got a clear shot," she declared.

"Lilly, I can't pull this off without you," begged
Miley. "Come on. Help me."

I can't believe it, Miley thought. Every other kid
here gets to sit around the campfire, toasting
marshmallows. And what do I get? *Dishpan hands!*

Oliver sighed. "I have to share a tent with Donny tonight. He had *five* helpings of beans!"

Lilly, Oliver and Miley hid in the bushes and laughed as they watched Amber and Ashley race straight to the Porta-John.

"Looks like my daddy was wrong," said Miley.
"I got down with the dogs and got up *flea free*."

fun. I do it all the time."

Mr Picker raised an eyebrow. "Little Miley Sunshine, trying to turn my frown upside down?"

Miley nodded. Then, just for good measure, she threw the man one of her dazzling Hannah Montana grins. Now if *that* don't take the grump out of the guy, she thought, I'll eat my glitter sunglasses.

"That's very sweet," Mr Picker told her, "and, at this moment, *incredibly annoying*!"

Miley frowned. So much for that, she thought. And I am *not* eating my sunglasses, thank you very much.

"Now get your parents to sign these forms," Mr Picker told the class as he pulled them out of his briefcase. "So you can spend twenty-four glorious hours with me and *no* indoor plumbing."

"Ewwww!" cried Amber and Ashley.

Miley rolled her eyes. *Princess alert*, she thought. But then, it figures the prissy twins would be grossed out. They'd probably never even *seen* an outside toilet before, let alone used one.

Miley, on the other hand, didn't have any problem with the great outdoors. She loved camping and she'd had plenty of experience with the no-flush throne. In fact, according to her dad, one of their distant relatives still lived – as he put it – the 'rustic' life back home in Tennessee. Translation: he had an outside toilet.

Of course, the A-for-Attitude girls were far from happy about the idea. As Mr Picker started passing out the permission forms, they began complaining.

"I don't want to go to the toilet in the woods," Ashley whined.

"I don't even like going *here*!" Amber cried.

Miley spoke up, hoping she could change their minds.

"Just think about it," she drawled in her country-girl voice. "Campin' under the stars, breathin' all that fresh mountain air, surrounded by the sounds o' nature . . ." Miley paused to create some convincing sound effects – bird whistles, owl hoots and chipmunk calls.

Amber and Ashley shuddered.

"*What* are you doing?" Amber snapped.

Miley threw up her hands. "A chipmunk, *duh*," she replied.

Amber made a disgusted face. Ashley lifted her chin. "Could you *be* any more of a hillbilly?" she asked.

Miley shook her head and thought, if that girl's nose gets stuck any higher, she'll be sniffing the ceiling!

"Well, I could've done a pig," she told them, "but you guys have already got that covered."

As Amber and Ashley spluttered, trying (and failing) to think of a comeback, Lilly joined in the fun.

"Mmm, what's that I smell?" she asked wryly. "Bacon that just got *burned*!"

Ashley narrowed her eyes. "Geeks," she spat.

"Freaks," Miley countered.

Amber and Ashley pointed their fingers first at Miley, next at Lilly. "Loser! . . . Loser! . . . Ooh!" they cried. Then they touched their fingers together and made a *sizzle* sound.

Like they're hot, Miley thought. *Not!*

"Do that stupid finger thing one more time," threatened Lilly with a raised fist, "and I will—"

Just then, Miley noticed Mr Picker walking towards them with his permission forms.

"Ooh, catfight on aisle five," he declared.

Miley gulped, seeing visions of detention dancing in her head – along with a *cancelled* Hannah rehearsal!

"Sir," she quickly jumped in, trying to save the situation, "we were just talking about what a kick it was going to be to get to know each other better." She bobbed her head so hard she felt like a dashboard ornament. "Right, guys?"

Lilly, Amber and Ashley followed her lead. Now they all looked like bobble-headed dolls!

"Oh, yeah!" they cried. "You bet! . . . Uh-huh!"

"Good," said Mr Picker. "You're sharing

the same tent."

"*WHAT?*" the girls cried together.

Miley had seen group hugs. But she'd never before witnessed group *horror* – until now!

"Oh, you don't *want* to share the same tent?" Mr Picker asked, looking all concerned.

For a second, the girls felt relieved. They were sure the teacher was going to reassign them. But, with a look of twisted glee, Mr Picker said, "Even better!"

Then he slapped the forms on their desks, turned to Miley and asked, "How do you like camping *now*, chipmunk?"

Chapter Two

On the day of the camping trip, Miley got up extra early. She heard a familiar deep voice floating up from downstairs.

To anyone else, it would have sounded as if Robby Stewart was working on a new hit tune for Hannah Montana. But Mr Stewart was more than Miley's songwriter and manager. He was also her father. And Miley had his number. She knew *exactly* what he was doing in their living room.

"Ninety-eight . . . I see ya," Mr Stewart

sang, ". . . ninety-nine . . . I'm coming to get'cha . . . one hundred. Come 'ere, darlin', time to dance!"

Miley's dad finished his one hundred sit-ups and snatched his reward – the gooey piece of cake on the coffee table.

Still in her pyjamas, Miley watched from the top of the stairs. *Perfect*, she thought. *Now that Dad's all sugared up, this will be easy!*

She uncapped her red marker pen and drew a few more little red dots on her face and arms. Then she tossed the marker away.

Fake rash in place, she thought. *Check!* *And now for the fake coughing spell.*

Cough-cough . . . cough-cough . . . cough-cough-cough! She hacked as she moved down the stairs.

Her dad hadn't noticed yet, but Miley kept it up. *The trick is in the rhythm*, she figured. Just like any good Hannah performance. *Cough-cough . . . cough-cough . . . cough-cough-cough!*

"Hey, buddy," said Mr Stewart, licking icing off his fingers, "you look terrible."

"Couldn't sleep," said Miley in a fake raspy voice. "Feel sick." And now for the death rattle she'd been practising for the last half hour.

"Whoa," said her father, hearing Miley's laboured breathing. "You sound like that donkey who used to carry fat Uncle Earl up the hill to church . . . and look at that rash! There's no way you're going on that camping trip today."

"But Daddy," said Miley, pausing to cough some more. "I'm fine."

Miley swayed as if she were really dizzy. Then she dramatically fell on the sofa. *Wow!* she thought. I deserve an Oscar for this performance!

Miley's dad looked very concerned. He put a hand on her forehead. "Sorry, darlin'," he said, gravely shaking his head. "You're going back to bed."

As he turned away, Miley bit her lip to keep from singing out, *Vic-to-ry!*

"I'll just have to cancel that interview," said Miley's dad, reaching for the phone. "You know, the one Hannah Montana was going to give Taylor Kingsford?"

"Taylor Kingsford?!" Miley leaped to her feet and yanked the phone out of her father's hand. "He's the coolest VJ on TV! This is awesome!"

Miley's dad raised an eyebrow. The gravely ill girl was *apparently* no longer woozy, raspy or weak. In fact, she looked fit as a fiddle.

Suddenly, Miley realized what she'd

done. She tried to cough again. But now *she* knew that *he* knew exactly what was going on.

"Nice try," her father quipped. "But next time you might want to go for a *waterproof* rash." He held up the hand that he'd placed on her forehead. There were red stains all over his palm.

Miley gulped. "I'm healed," she tried weakly. "Hallelujah?"

Mr Stewart folded his arms. "Miley, I know you don't want to share a tent with Amber and Ashley, but sometimes you've just got to make the best of a bad situation."

"Well, in that case," said Miley, "I'm going to need a jar of honey, a thousand red ants and the cover of nightfall!"

"Times like this, you remind me of your mum," said Mr Stewart.

Miley's mother had passed away three

years before. And he often told Miley how much she took after her.

"Look, Mile," said Mr Stewart. "I know those girls don't treat you right, but sinking down to their level isn't the answer."

Miley tapped her chin, thinking it over. "How do we really know that until we *try*?"

Mr Stewart shook his head. "Remember that kid back home who always teased Jackson, so Jackson sneaked into his bathroom to glue his toilet seat?"

Oh, yeah, Miley remembered. Her older brother Jackson had plenty of ideas, but not a lot of common sense. The bullying kid never knew what happened. But Jackson came home with his blond hair soaking wet, a toilet seat glued to his forehead and a screwdriver glued to his hand.

"It would've worked if I hadn't slipped!" her brother had wailed.

Miley laughed at the memory. "He sure brightened up that crowd in the emergency room!"

"Aw, good times, good times," her father agreed. Then he cleared his throat and refocused. "My *point* is, when you lie down with dogs, you're going to get up with fleas."

"Not if I wear a flea collar!" Miley argued.

Mr Stewart sighed. He could see he just wasn't getting through to his little girl. So he sat her down and looked straight into her eyes. "Mile," he said firmly, "I'm asking you as a favour to be the *better person* here."

Miley gritted her teeth in frustration. "But I already *am* the better person, why do I have to act like it?"

"*Promise* me," her father insisted.

Miley sighed in defeat. She could see her dad was all too serious about this. "Okay, fine," she promised.

Mr Stewart smiled. "That's my girl!"

DING, DING, DING, DING, DING!

Miley and her father jumped at the sound of the burglar alarm going off.

Was there a break-in? Miley wondered.

Mr Stewart raced to the back door. But the door was closed and the lock was set.

"Aw, man!" he cried, realizing what had happened. "That dang mouse is chewing on the wires again!"

Miley watched her dad stomp to the kitchen and grab a frying pan. "That's it," he exclaimed, raising the pan. "I'm going to—"

"Oh, no, you're not!" Miley squealed, leaping in front of her dad. "That mouse is a living creature. I've even given it a name . . . *Linda*. It's Spanish for 'pretty'."

"Well," replied Mr Stewart, "you'd better start learning the Spanish for 'squished'!"

Chapter Three

Oliver Oken was ready for the great outdoors. He had his big-game hunter's vest. He had his bushman's hat. He had his video camera. And, most importantly of all, he had his fake Australian accent.

"It was the sixth day without food," he declared. "Only one man could guide the remaining survivors to safety. Oliver Oscar Oken. The Triple O – known the world over as *Ooo*."

Miley rolled her eyes. Oliver had been

recording himself on video since they'd piled on to the school bus. Now that they'd arrived at the campsite, she'd just about had it with the crocodile-hunter act.

"Knock it off, Ooo!" she told him.

But Oliver was just getting started. He swung the camera around to focus on Miley's face. "It's the Malibu Miley cat!" he cried. "Very rare, very vicious!"

Suddenly, the camera was yanked from Oliver's hands. It was Donny. He turned the camera around to film Oliver.

"And this is the Dorkus Oliverus!" he exclaimed. "Very rare, very stupid."

Donny cackled with his posse of friends. "You hear that? *Dorkus Oliverus*! 'Cause he's a dork." Donny slapped his knee. "I'm on fire!"

Oliver snatched his camera back. But before he could say anything to Donny,

Mr Picker began to clap his hands.

"Okay, people," the teacher announced, "time for another pop quiz. Could there possibly be a better place to study nature?"

As Oliver began to raise his hand, Milo grimaced. He had seen Oliver fall for the 'pop quiz' game too many times to count.

"No!" Milo cried, lunging to pull down Oliver's arm.

Mr Picker pointed at Milo. "Wrong," he said.

Milo smacked his forehead.

"The answer is *yes*," declared Mr Picker. "There is a better place to study nature – on a forty-two-inch, high-def, plasma-screen TV in my den – steps away from *indoor* plumbing!" To make his point, the teacher glanced at the campsite's Porta-John and shuddered.

"Come on, Mr Picker," said Miley,

stepping up. "You can't enjoy the smell and feel of nature on your TV."

"That's the whole point," he replied, slapping an insect off his arm. "Now set up your tents and get into them where I can't see you. And, remember, if you have any questions, pray for a forest ranger, 'cause that's what I'll be doing."

Like the other kids, Miley took off her rucksack and picked out a spot to set up her tent. The campsite itself was very pretty. Large, old trees and flowering bushes surrounded a clearing of low grass. Miley could hear the birds singing and the familiar burbling of a nearby creek.

Here's a good spot, she thought. Better get to it. She started removing the tent from its canvas bag, when she felt a hard tap on her shoulder. She looked up to find Lilly pointing across the clearing.

"There they are," she whispered.

Amber and Ashley were sitting under a tree, comparing nail-varnish shades. Miley's tentmates were obviously skiving off the work of setting up their home away from home.

Lilly pulled a catapult out of her pocket. "I've got a clear shot," she declared.

"Lilly, wait," Miley said, stepping in front of her, "you could get into trouble. Let me handle this."

Lilly thought it over. "Okay," she finally agreed, "but make it *hurt*."

Miley sighed. "You can count on that," she promised. Then she approached Amber and Ashley, remembering what her father had said. I'm not supposed to sink to their level, she reminded herself.

"Okay," she told the girls, "I know we've had our problems, but Lilly and I are willing to forget all that if you are—"

A hard yank on her arm interrupted her. It was Lilly, pulling her away. "I thought you said it was going to hurt!" she hissed.

"Trust me," said Miley. "It was the most painful thing I've ever done. But I promised my dad I'd be the better person."

"Well, I didn't!" Lilly noted. She lifted her catapult again.

"Lilly, I can't pull this off without you," begged Miley. "Come on. Help me."

Lilly folded her arms. "Why?"

"Because," said Miley, "you're my friend."

"No," she said.

"Then help me because it's the right thing to do," Miley pleaded.

"*Ohhhh*, no," said Lilly.

"Then help me because . . . I'm on *The Taylor Kingsford Show* tomorrow night," said Miley. "And if you don't, I'm not taking you."

Lilly's eyes widened and her jaw dropped. Two seconds later, she was swooping down on Amber and Ashley with a huge, fake smile. "Hello, tent pals!" she cheerfully exclaimed. "Who wants me to plait their hair?"

Amber and Ashley grimaced at Lilly's grubby tomboy fingers. "Ewww!" they cried.

Miley stepped up and put on her own fake smile – which, she discovered, was a *whole* lot harder than putting on a fake rash.

"Oh, come on," she said. "Whaddya say we put up this tent, make a fire and cook us up a big pot of friendship?"

Ashley rolled her eyes. "We'd like to," she told Miley, "but we don't speak *Hillbilly*."

"Or do our washing down yonder in the *crick*," Amber added.

Miley remembered her promise to her dad. Clenching her fists, she forced herself to laugh. Elbowing Lilly, she got her best friend to join in.

"I hate them," Lilly whispered to Miley through fake chuckles.

"Taylor Kingsford, Taylor Kingsford," Miley quietly reminded her between her own fake ha-has.

Ashley and Amber narrowed their eyes with suspicion at the laughing Miley and Lilly. Then they rudely turned away.

"You know what I'm thinking, Ash?" said Amber.

"Half-caff-" said Ashley.

"-nonfat-" added Amber.

"-grande-latte-with-just-a-sprinkle-winkle-of-cinnamon. Ooh," the girls said together. Then they touched fingers as if they were on fire. "Ssss . . ."

Lilly couldn't take it. As the prissy pair headed towards a forest footpath, she pulled out her catapult again. "That's it," she told Miley, taking aim. "I'm going to sprinkle their winkles!"

"No! Remember Taylor Kingsford!" cried Miley. She lunged to spoil Lilly's aim just as the girl released her shot.

"Ow!" cried Mr Picker.

Miley cringed. She'd spoiled Lilly's aim, all right. The shot had missed Amber and Ashley – and hit their teacher!

Luckily for them, the man had been bending over at the time.

"That's a bite!" exclaimed the teacher. He'd already been freaking out over the insects. Now he grabbed his stinging rear end and cried, "That's a *big* bite."

Chapter Four

While Miley's teacher thought he was being bitten, Miley's father and brother were trying to *get* a bite. They'd set a trap – complete with some delicious cheese – to catch the mouse. But somehow the mouse had stolen the cheese from right under their noses!

Mr Stewart clenched his fists. Losing was something he had always taken in his stride. But losing to a rodent was *humiliating*!

Meanwhile, back at camp, Miley's best friend was having a meltdown.

"Well, this is just great!" Lilly cried. "Amber and Ashley bail and now we have to put this thing up all by ourselves!"

Lilly was so angry, she couldn't even look at Miley. She just paced back and forth, staring at the ground. "I mean, ask me to change the trucks on a skateboard. I can do that. But a tent? This'll take forever!"

When Lilly finally looked up, she saw Miley standing next to a fully assembled tent. Lilly's jaw dropped. The thing was so perfectly put together, it could have been a display model in a camping shop!

"How did you—" she began.

But Miley waved her hand. "When you're raised in Tennessee, they teach you

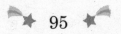

this before you're potty trained," she said. "Look inside, there's cut flowers."

As Lilly looked inside, Miley heard a commotion nearby. Together, she and Lilly followed the noise. They found a tangle of fabric, poles and ropes on the ground – and two boys arguing in the middle of it.

"Donny," said Oliver, "I don't think it goes that way."

"You should've stopped that sentence after 'I don't think'!" Donny declared. Then he turned to his crew of friends. "Did you hear that? 'I don't think!' 'Cause he *doesn't think*! . . . I own him!"

Donny's followers laughed. And Oliver clenched his fists. "Yeah," he shot back at Donny, "well, *you* should've stopped after . . . uh, 'Did you hear that?' Did you hear that?"

Milo stepped up to Oliver. "They heard

it," he whispered. "That's why they're not laughing."

Oliver frowned. Okay, he thought, so my insult made absolutely no sense. So what! I'm going to put this tent up *my* way!

He grabbed one end of the spring-loaded fabric and pulled it towards him. But Donny wasn't about to let Oliver win. So he grabbed the other end.

"Oh, come on," Donny taunted, "you can pull harder than that, Olivia!"

Oliver narrowed his eyes. "Oh, you're going to regret that, Don . . . na!"

Lilly giggled at that. But Miley wasn't laughing. She could see the boys needed a referee. With the tent frame bowing all the way to the ground, she moved over it and stood right between them.

"Step aside, rookies," she confidently declared. "Let me show you how to do this."

But Oliver didn't step aside. Instead, he pulled his end harder. "I can do it if he'd just let go!"

Donny shook his head. "You let go!"

Just then, both Donny and Oliver lost their grips. The tent flipped upwards and Miley was caught in the middle.

"Tent wedgie, tent wedgie!" she cried. The spring-loaded contraption snapped up between her legs and left her hanging upside down.

This is bad, she thought, holding on tight. But it could be worse. And a minute later, it *was*. Amber and Ashley returned from their wilderness walk.

"Nowhere to buy a latte," whined Amber, "nowhere to buy shoes and not a single multiplex. Why would anyone want to come to the woods?"

Ashley nodded in agreement. "It's

nothing but trees. What a waste of space!"

Just then, the two girls noticed the tent that Miley had put up. "Are we supposed to sleep in this?" Amber asked. She ran her hand over the fabric. "It's synthetic!"

"Ewwww." The two girls cringed in horror.

Miley rolled her eyes, watching the prissy pair from her upside-down perch. She almost didn't see Mr Picker walking right up to her.

"What are you doing?" the teacher asked.

Duh, thought Miley. Isn't it obvious? "Pitching a tent," she replied.

Mr Picker raised an eyebrow. "How's that working out for you?"

Miley shrugged. "I'm hangin' in there."

"Great," said the teacher, throwing up

his hands. "I have so many bites on my tush, it looks like a waffle."

"Yoo-hoo, Mr Picker?" called Amber, waving her hand.

When the teacher looked over, Ashley pointed to the tent Miley had erected and asked, "Did we build *ours* the right way?"

"What?!" cried Miley. She was so shocked by Ashley's lie that she let go of her perch and dropped like a rock.

Dang, that hurts, Miley thought as she scrambled to her feet. But Mr Picker had already gone to check out her tent.

"Wow, I'm impressed," he told Amber and Ashley. "You should see mine. I threw it in the lake."

"But *Miley* put up that tent!" Lilly cried, running over to defend her best friend. "*They* just went for lattes!"

Amber and Ashley threw Lilly a look

of total disbelief. "Lattes?" Amber repeated.

"In the forest?!" Ashley cried.

Then Amber shook her head. "I can't believe you would try to take credit for something we did."

"All we wanted to do was put up a tent, make a fire and cook us up a big pot of friendship," Ashley proclaimed.

"That's what I said!" Miley cried.

But Amber wasn't about to admit it. "She's taking credit again!" she whined. "Mr Picker, make her stop."

Mr Picker put a hand to his throbbing head. "If it'll make *you* stop, sure," he told her. "Here's a thought: why don't you just apologize to each other, or at the very least fake an illness so we can all *go home*."

Miley could see she'd been trumped.

Choking back her anger, she spat out, "Fine . . . I'm sorry."

Now it was Lilly's turn to apologize. But by now she was so angry that she was actually shaking. Miley nudged her and Lilly finally opened her mouth.

"Right," said Lilly. "We're both sorry . . . that you two are evil, lying loads of *nasty*!"

That evening, Miley and Lilly were not happy campers. Mr Picker had assigned the two to KP duty. Miley didn't know what those letters meant, but she suspected the *P* stood for pain in the neck!

She and Lilly were stuck cleaning all the plates, cups and utensils the students used at dinner. I can't believe it, Miley thought, bent over a bowl of soapsuds. Every other kid here gets to sit around the campfire, toasting marshmallows. And what do I get?

Dishpan hands!

"A little tip," Mr Picker told Lilly as he handed her his empty coffee cup. "In the future, when apologizing, leave out the phrase, 'lying loads of *nasty*'."

Suppressing a chuckle, the teacher headed back to the campfire. A minute later, Oliver walked over and handed Miley his dinner plate.

"Here," he said.

Miley washed the dish. Then Lilly dried it and placed it on the mile-high stack they'd already cleaned. That's when Miley noticed that Oliver hadn't returned to the campfire. He just stood there, looking almost as miserable as she felt.

"What's your problem?" Miley asked.

Oliver sighed. "I have to share a tent with Donny tonight."

"So?" asked Lilly.

"He had *five* helpings of beans!" Oliver exclaimed.

"Oh, come on, Oliver," said Miley, "it's not like he did it on purpose."

"I think he *did*," Oliver replied, pointing at the campfire. Donny was grinning in their direction. With one hand, he pointed at Oliver. With the other, he fanned his rear end.

Defeated, Oliver returned to the campfire. Amber and Ashley approached Miley and Lilly.

"Look, we feel bad about this," Amber began. "We didn't know he'd make you wash all the dishes."

"But, look, you've *almost* finished," said Ashley. Then she dropped her plate into the bowl and accidentally-on-purpose knocked over their tower of clean plates.

"Oops, sorry," Ashley said. "See? I can apologize."

Amber put an arm around her friend's shoulders. "Well, that's because *you're* the bigger person."

As the two walked away, laughing, Miley turned to Lilly. Too outraged to say a word, she grabbed Lilly's hand, slapped it over her own mouth and screamed into it. Then she calmly removed her friend's hand and said, "Thank you."

"Forget Taylor Kingsford," Lilly told Miley in a calm voice. "I'm going after them and don't try to stop me."

"Who's stopping you? I'm going with you!" Miley declared. That prissy pair had finally gone too far. "Sorry, Dad," she whispered. "Get the flea powder ready, 'cause tonight I'm lyin' down with the dogs."

Chapter Five

As night fell over the forest, the stars came out. The students went into their tents. And, without a word to each other, Miley, Lilly, Amber and Ashley climbed into their sleeping bags.

Just as they were dozing off, a loud rustling sound outside awoke Amber. "What was that?" she whispered. Sitting up in alarm, she turned on her torch. "Ashley . . . Ashley!"

Ashley was dreaming about a typical day

at school. "Move your hand," she mumbled. "I can't see your answers."

As the rustling continued, Amber smacked her friend on the shoulder.

"Ow!" cried Ashley, finally waking up.

Lilly rolled over. "What's going on?" she asked through a yawn.

"I heard something outside," Amber whispered.

Miley waved her hand. "It was probably just the wind–" suddenly, she heard a low, guttural growl, "– or not," Miley revised with a gulp. She quickly sat up and so did Lilly.

By this time, Amber and Ashley were close to terrified. "Mr Picker!" they called in a strangled whisper. "Mr Picker!"

Mr Picker's tent wasn't far away, but there was no way he was going to hear Amber and Ashley calling. The man had slapped a sleep mask over his eyes and stuck ear plugs in his ears.

"Just hold it in, Picker," he chanted to himself, "twelve more hours, you can do it..."

Meanwhile, in Miley's tent, things went from bad to worse. The menacing growl had grown louder and closer.

"What is that thing?!" Amber cried.

"Don't know," said Miley, her eyes widening. "Could be a bear, a mountain lion . . ."

Lilly looked scared, too. "Whatever it is, it sounds hungry."

GRRRRRRRRR! BAM!

Something powerful struck the tent. It swayed back and forth like a carnival ride, and Amber and Ashley totally freaked out.

"I'm too pretty to get eaten!" Ashley squealed.

She tried to shove Amber in front of her. But Amber protested. "Hey," she said, "I'm pretty, too!"

"I'll mention that at your funeral!" Ashley promised, still struggling to throw her best friend to the wolves, the lions, or whatever other wild animals were out there!

Miley couldn't take it any more. She kicked off her sleeping bag and got to her feet.

"Miley, what are you doing?" Lilly asked.

"If we stay in here, we'll get torn to pieces," Miley replied. "Our only hope is if I can get to the ranger station alive."

Lilly violently shook her head. "Miley, this is stupid. I just can't let you go."

"But, *we* can!" cried Amber.

"Go, go!" Ashley urged Miley. "Be stupid!"

Before Lilly could stop her, Miley was moving to the tent's front flap. "Don't worry," she said, halfway out. "I'm going to be just *f-i-i-i-i-i-i-i-ne*!"

Amber and Ashley screamed as Miley was yanked right out of their midst.

On the other side of the tent, Miley whispered, "Thanks for the help."

Oliver shrugged. "Anything to get out of Donny's tent," he said. "He got a standing ovation from the skunks."

"Ready?" she whispered.

He nodded and lifted the stick in his hand. Then Oliver began to make growling and yelping sounds.

"Oh, no, you don't!" Miley cried.

Oliver beat the tent with his stick.

"Yeah, that's right!" Miley called. "Not so tough now . . ."

A second later, Oliver broke the stick.

"Ow, my leg!" Miley squealed.

Oliver picked up a second stick and

broke it.

"And my other leg!" she cried.

Oliver broke a third stick and Miley glared at him. "And my arm!" she added, but thought, *enough already!*

Meanwhile, back inside the tent, Amber and Ashley were having a total meltdown. Amber grabbed Lilly by the shoulders. "Okay, you go next," she demanded.

"Why me?" squeaked Lilly.

Ashley rolled her eyes. "I think we've established the 'pretty scale'."

Lilly glared at them, but they didn't care. When Miley's head appeared through a flap in the back of the tent, they shrank back in horror.

"Lilly, he's got me!" Miley exclaimed.

"Oh no, he hasn't!" Lilly cried. She tried to pull Miley back inside. But it was no use.

"It's too late," Miley called. "Goodbye!" Her head disappeared and the girls heard her scream, "Ahhhh!"

Lilly freaked out. "No, Miley, no!" She pushed her own head through the back flap. "Hey! You let her go, you – *whoa*!"

Lilly was pulled right out of the tent. Amber and Ashley stared in shock. The growling, snarling animal that had eaten Miley had just got Lilly, too!

Outside, hiding in the bushes, Miley, Lilly and Oliver bit their tongues to keep from laughing. Then they stepped out of the bushes, found some tree branches and began to beat the tent.

Amber and Ashley came flying out of their synthetic fortress, screaming like crazed Hannah Montana fans. But there was no encore needed at this performance.

They raced straight to the Porta-John, fighting with each other to get inside. But when they pulled open the door, they found Donny inside. The baron of beans was washing his hands.

"Hey! *Occupado*!" Donny protested.

Amber and Ashley didn't care. They forced their way inside and closed the door.

"Get out!" Donny demanded.

"You get out!" Ashley shrieked.

The Porta-John began to rock violently back and forth until it finally fell over. "Ahhhhhh!" they all screamed. Then came a great big, grossed-out "Ewwwwwww!"

Miley, Lilly and Oliver celebrated with high fives. Lilly grinned as she pulled out her camera phone and took aim.

"Looks like my daddy was wrong," said Miley, posing in front of the toilet. "I got down with the dogs and got up *flea free*."

Chapter Six

The next afternoon, VJ Taylor Kingsford was just about ready to interview Hannah Montana.

"And that was Hannah Montana's latest pop video!" he announced to the television camera. "Stick around, in a minute we'll be back with the real deal. I love you! I mean it!"

A second later, the stage manager called, "And we're clear!"

With his show in a commercial break,

Taylor walked over to Miley. She was waiting in the wings.

"There you are," he called, "looking fine!"

Dressed in her long, blonde Hannah wig, cool sunglasses and glittery clothes, Miley smiled a big smile.

"And who's your wing-woman?" Taylor asked.

Standing right beside Miley was Lilly, although no one would be able to tell; she was dressed in her Lola Luftnagle disguise.

Lilly stared wide-eyed at Taylor for a minute. Then she began to giggle hysterically.

Taylor leaned towards Miley. "Is she all right?" he whispered.

Miley shook her head. "I ask myself that question every day." Just then, her mobile phone rang. She answered the call. It was Oliver.

"What do you want?" she asked impatiently. "I'm almost on."

Oliver was calling from his bathroom, where he'd been slathering his legs and arms with calamine lotion.

"Listen, Miley, this is important!" he told her. "Remember that bush we were standing in outside your tent? It was poison oak!"

"That's crazy. If it was, I'd be—" Miley froze, "—doing *this*!"

And what was 'this'? *Scratching!* Miley suddenly realized she'd been scratching her arms for the last few minutes.

"Baby girl," called Taylor from the TV set, "if you want to be on the *show*, you need to be on the *stage*."

"Got to go," Miley told Oliver. She snapped her phone closed and crossed the stage to her seat.

"Okay," she whispered to herself,

waiting for the stage manager's signal, "this scratching is just in my head. It's just because he said it. I mean, Lilly isn't–"

She glanced offstage and saw Lilly desperately trying to scratch her own back. The girl was rubbing against a piece of the stage set like a bear against a tree!

Uh-oh, thought Miley, feeling the exact same itch begin to tickle her, too. This is *so* not good.

"We're back," the stage manager warned, "in three, two . . ."

"And we're back with Hannah Montana," said Taylor Kingsford. "Hannah, welcome. I'm just itching to ask you a few questions."

"And I'm *itching* to answer them," she said, squirming in her seat. If only you could do us both a favour, she thought, and *scratch* it for me!

"You always come across as so . . .

squeaky clean," said Taylor. "Now let's be real, is that the true Hannah Montana?"

Miley swallowed hard. The itching was spreading all over – her arms, her legs, her face. But the absolute worst was her back!

"Well," she said, struggling to concentrate on answering Taylor's question, "I've always believed that at the end of the day it's about loving others–" she spread her arms out wide, "–as you would love yourself."

"Boring!" Taylor replied as Miley quickly brought her arms back in to scratch them.

"Come on," he challenged, "haven't you ever sunk down and done something . . . b-a-a-a-d?"

"Yes," she confessed, rubbing her itchy back against the back of her chair. "And I learned . . . *just recently* . . . that when you lie down with dogs you *do* get up with fleas!"

"Are you okay?" asked Taylor, seeing his guest begin to claw her neck like a flea-bitten puppy.

"Never better!" Miley lied. "I've just been, uh . . . working on a new dance routine . . ." She scratched some more. "And I can't wait to show you."

Taylor grinned big and faced the camera. "How about that? A Taylor Kingsford sneaky peek!"

"First I need a beat. Give me that mike!" Miley demanded.

She put the microphone to her mouth, as if she were about to start singing. But the itch became so bad she started using it as a back scratcher.

ZIP-ZIP! . . . ZIP-ZIP-ZIP! . . . ZIP-ZIP!

"Oh, yeah, oh, yeah," said Miley in relief.

But to Taylor, it sounded like a hip-hop beat. "Come on, band," he called, bobbing his head to her back-scratching rhythms, "help her out!"

ZIP-ZIP! . . . ZIP-ZIP-ZIP! . . . ZIP-ZIP!

"Contagious, isn't it?" said Miley. "Everybody's doing it! See?"

Miley ran offstage and dragged Lilly back on to help her out. "I call it the scratch dance!" she cried. She handed Lilly the mike. "A little to the left," she instructed her, "now a little to the right, higher, lower, that's just right! Oh, yeah, oh, yeah, scratch dancin'! Don't stop now! Scratch dancin'!"

"Now switch!" Lilly cried, desperate to get her own itch taken care of.

"You wish!" said Miley. "Scratch dancin'! Scratch dancin'!"

* * *

That night, Miley sat in front of her television, covered in calamine lotion – and shame. "I can't watch this," she told her dad, hiding her eyes.

Her appearance on Taylor Kingsford's show had been taped earlier. Now it was being replayed for the whole country, including her father and brother. And both of them thought the scratch dance was a riot.

"You don't have to watch it," Miley's father told her with a chuckle. "I'm *recording* it. I never get tired of watching me being right."

Jackson jumped up and imitated her dance with silly, exaggerated moves. "Scratch dancin'! Scratch dancin'!" he squealed. "It *is* contagious!"

"If you don't stop it, you're going to find out!" Miley warned her brother.

Jackson refused to stop, so Miley took off after him. Spreading her rash-covered arms wide, she was just *itching* to give him a nice, big hug!

You'd better run, Jackson, she thought, because even if my dance isn't contagious, I'm pretty sure my poison oak is!

Put your hands together
for the next Hannah
Montana book . . .

Adapted by M.C. King

Based on the television series *Hannah Montana*, created by Michael Poryes and Rich Correll and Barry O'Brien

Based on the episode written by Lisa Albert

As Miley Stewart stared at the screen of her laptop computer, she could practically hear her best friend Lilly's heart beating. Lilly was Miley's confidante and constant companion and right now she was reading over Miley's shoulder. "This is so cool!" Lilly yelped, "I can't believe how many people email Hannah Montana."

From the look of it, Miley appeared to be an average eighth grader. But Miley, mild-mannered junior-high-school student by day, had a secret. She was also Hannah Montana, pop superstar. Only a few people knew that Miley was the normal girl behind mega-successful Hannah's awesome disguise. Lilly was one of them.

Miley read off the computer screen: "Dear Hannah, you rock. Jill in Milwaukee."

So sweet!

"Dear Hannah, you're awesome! Danny in Iowa City."

Cool.

Hi, I'm Hannah Montana!

There aren't a lot of people who know that when I'm not Hannah Montana, I'm actually Miley Stewart, a normal American teenager. Only my closest friends know my secret, and of course, my family do too. Although they never treat me like I'm a superstar - to them, I'm just Miley!

My family used to live in Tennessee. But a while back, we moved to Malibu, California, which is slammin. It has awesome beaches and it hardly ever rains here! I live with my big brother Jackson, and my dad, Robby Stewart. Dad does a great job looking after Jackson and me. Sometimes though, Dad can be way over-protective and thinks I'm still a little girl!

My family are kind of crazy, but I still love them. Wanna know more? Well read on and I'll tell you all about them!

Loads of love,

Hannah xx

Monday

Dear Diary

I've got a secret! Most people would never believe that an ordinary teenager like me would secretly be a popstar like Hannah Montana!

This week looks like it should be fantastic! I've finally got some time off from being a celebrity! I'm going to do regular, everyday stuff, like hanging out with my best friends, Lilly and Oliver.

It isn't all cool, though. I've got tons of homework to do! My maths assignment is going to take FOREVER. My dad is really big on studying, and I know it's important, too. But I like to do my homework in all kinds of weird places, I once studied on a skateboard!

Tuesday

Amber and Ashley are two of the meanest girls at Seaview Middle School. Today they were going on about how much they rate Hannah Montana. But they're always really horrible to me! They'd freak if they knew I was Hannah!

Ashley said Hannah had written to her, inviting her and Amber to hang out. What a big fat lie! I haven't written them anything. Ashley showed me one of the letters, but looked really dumb when I pointed out it was her handwriting!

When I got home, some photos from a shoot I did last week had arrived for me to check out. Crazy poses, huh?!

Wednesday

After school today, Dad took Jackson and me to the movies. We saw this funny film, and I ate a huge tub of popcorn. Yum! After the movie, we grabbed a pizza. It was totally embarrassing, because in the restaurant they were playing my new album. Cringesome!

Sometimes it's nice just to hang out with my family. We've done all kinds of rockin' stuff in the past.

Like any big brother, Jackson can be annoying. He always teases me! But tonight he was pretty cool. It was an awesome night!

Robby (dad)

Me, Miley

Thursday

Lilly came round before school today, and I was still in bed! She wanted to borrow some of my clothes.

We looked through my Hannah Montana wardrobe (which is a lot sassier than my Miley wardrobe). I've got an awesome clothing rack that spins around, so I can check out my leather jackets, denim jackets, mini-skirts, jeans and heaps of great boots and shoes.

We tried on so many different outfits! We were going to wear these really cool short skirts and tank tops but when Dad saw us, he said there was no way we were wearing those clothes to school. Major spoilsport!

Friday

I have a crush on a boy at school. He's new here, and his name is Jake. It's so exciting having a crush on someone! I wonder if he likes me too...

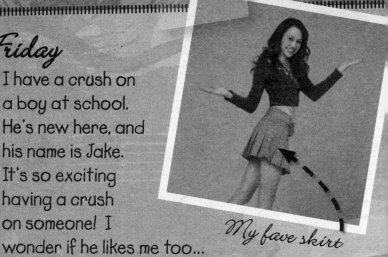

My fave skirt

We've been hanging out together at Seaview.

Oliver used to have a crush on Hannah Montana, but then he found out Hannah was me! We're really good friends, so his crush disappeared super quickly!

Saturday and Sunday

One of the coolest things about living in Malibu is that you're never too far away from the beach! Lilly, Oliver and I decided to hit the surf this weekend.

After some chillin' on the beach, we went to see Jackson at Rico's, the beach hangout where he works. It's an awesome snack shack – even though Rico is super annoying at times.

I still haven't forgotten the time Rico made me wear a chicken suit and paraglide along the beach. It was absolutely one of the most embarrassing moments of my life, mainly because I fell in the ocean and had to swim back to shore. Chicken suits are heavy when they're wet!

Fabulous Family WORDSEARCH!

Hunt out all the different names of relatives hidden in this word search grid. Words can go forwards, backwards, or diagonally.

Godmother ✓   Sister ✓   Uncle ✓
Grandfather   Mother ✓   Cousin ✓
Grandmother ✓ Aunt ✓   Father ✓
Brother

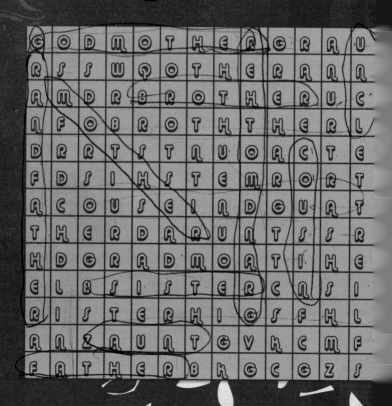

G	O	D	M	O	T	H	E	R	G	R	A	U
R	S	S	W	O	O	T	H	E	R	A	N	N
A	M	D	R	B	R	O	T	H	E	R	U	C
N	F	O	B	R	O	T	H	T	H	E	R	L
D	R	R	T	S	T	N	U	O	A	C	T	E
F	D	S	I	H	S	T	E	M	R	O	R	T
A	C	O	U	S	E	N	N	D	G	U	A	T
T	H	E	R	D	A	R	U	N	T	S	S	R
H	D	G	R	A	D	M	O	A	T	I	H	E
E	L	B	S	I	S	T	E	R	C	N	S	I
R	I	S	T	E	R	H	I	G	S	F	H	L
A	N	Z	A	U	N	T	G	V	H	C	M	F
F	A	T	H	E	R	B	R	G	C	G	Z	S

Hannah Montana's COOL CROSSWORD!

Need some time-out from your family? Then this awesome crossword will help keep you busy!

Across

4. Complete this Hannah Montana song: 'One in a ____'.
6. Roxy is Hannah's ____.
8. What is Jackson's surname?
9. Who is Ashley's best friend?

Down

1. Lilly and Miley are best ____.
2. Which country does Miley live in?
3. Miley Stewart has a secret identity. She's Hannah ____.
5. Lilly's disguise transforms her into ____ Luftnagle.
7. Unscramble these letters to reveal a character on the show: LVREOI

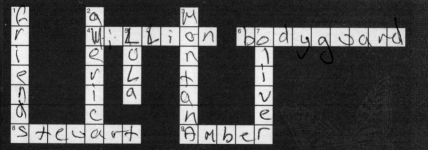

Hannah Montana's Chill Out Guide

Sometimes your family can get a bit too much. When your rellies are stressing you out, use this advice to chill, relax and stay calm...

Do some exercise. Go for a walk, or a run. It doesn't have to be very far – 15 or 20 minutes should do the trick.

Have a bath. Hit the tub, pop in some bubbles or bath oils, then just lie back and relax. Plus, you'll get to lock yourself away from the rest of your family!

Take time out to just 'be'. Lie down on your bed for ten minutes, and try to clear your mind of everything around you. Concentrate on thinking about nothing at all. Take slow, deep, calming breaths.

If you have a pet – play with it! Studies have shown that people with pets have lower stress levels. So walk your dog, stroke your cat, or cuddle up with your guinea pig. They'll love you for it too!

Put some of your favourite music on the stereo, close the curtains and then dance around like crazy! It'll instantly make you feel better – go on, really let rip!

Do something that makes you happy. Lilly enjoys surfing and skateboarding, while Hannah loves chilling with her guitar. It doesn't matter if it's sporty, musical or just reading a good book – doing anything you love will instantly make you feel better.

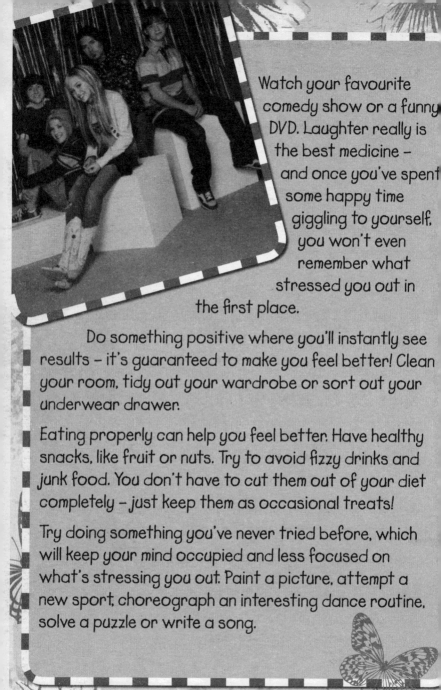

Watch your favourite comedy show or a funny DVD. Laughter really is the best medicine – and once you've spent some happy time giggling to yourself, you won't even remember what stressed you out in the first place.

Do something positive where you'll instantly see results – it's guaranteed to make you feel better! Clean your room, tidy out your wardrobe or sort out your underwear drawer.

Eating properly can help you feel better. Have healthy snacks, like fruit or nuts. Try to avoid fizzy drinks and junk food. You don't have to cut them out of your diet completely – just keep them as occasional treats!

Try doing something you've never tried before, which will keep your mind occupied and less focused on what's stressing you out. Paint a picture, attempt a new sport, choreograph an interesting dance routine, solve a puzzle or write a song.

WHAT KIND OF FAMILY ARE YOU?

The things you do with your family are probably very different to activities you do with your friends. But that's what makes family time so special! Take our quiz to find out what kind of family you have...

1. Describe how you'd spend a typical Saturday with your family:

A) Loafing at home, before getting together in the evening to watch some TV.

B) Playing football in the back garden, before going to a match.

C) Walking in the countryside.

2. How would you describe your family?

A) You do a lot of stuff on your own, but enjoy spending time together too.

B) Active and argumentative!

C) Pretty laid back and chilled out.

3. Your family has just celebrated with a massive birthday lunch. Where did you go?

A) You had a blow-out meal at home with all your favourite foods.

B) To a favourite local restaurant.

C) On a picnic.

4. What's your garden like?

A: A bit overgrown. The lawn only gets mowed when you're having a BBQ or want to do some sunbathing!

B: Covered in sports equipment, goal posts and basketball nets.

C: Quiet, pretty and well looked after.

5. How often do you exercise as a family?

A: Not very often.

B: All the time!

C: Usually only at the weekends.

6. What would be your perfect way of spending time as a family?

A: Board games, great snacks and a comedy DVD to watch.

B: Rounding up some friends and organizing team games in the park.

C: Heading out for a day at the beach.

MOSTLY As: You're Home Bodies!

Your family loves spending time together at home. Maybe you enjoy watching your favourite show on TV, having a movie night on the sofa, eating a meal together or playing board games, but you're happiest when you're under your own roof. Try not to get stuck in a rut though – sometimes it's nice to try different things, so why not suggest a trip to the cinema, or a weekend away?

MOSTLY Bs: You're Sports Fans!

Your family bond through its love of sports. You might go and watch football or rugby matches, play Frisbee in the park, or crowd around the TV watching a big game at home. It's great to have these shared interests – just be careful things don't get too competitive!

MOSTLY Cs: You're Nature Lovers!

You're a family that loves to spend time in the great outdoors. You enjoy walking, and appreciate wildlife and all the natural world has to offer. With all that exercise, you're definitely keeping healthy, and the fresh air will give your cheeks a rosy glow that's better than blusher any day!

This is the A – Z guide of all you need to know about Hannah Montana!

K is for Kickin' Dance Steps! I do loads of routines while I'm on stage, and have a special choreographer who works out the dance steps for me. I need to keep pretty fit to do all that bouncing about!

L is for Lilly. Lilly is one of my best friends. She found out that I was Hannah Montana when she snuck into my dressing room after a concert one night. Lilly has a disguise too, so nobody can tell it's her hanging around with me. She wears crazy wigs and adopts the persona of Lola Luftnagle.

M is for Music. Music is my life! I'm happiest when I'm singing, or writing songs, or dancing around. I like country and pop stuff best of all, but there's so much pumpin' stuff out there, everyone likes something. That's what's so great about it!

N is for Nerves. I always get nervous before I go on stage. It's a pretty big deal, performing in front of a crowd of thousands! But I have this routine now, where I jump around, shaking my nerves out, and making these weird monkey noises. It really seems to help.

O is for Oliver. Other than Lilly, Oliver is my best friend. He used to be madly in love with me (but only in my Hannah disguise). As soon as Oliver found out Hannah was actually his buddy Miley, his crush disappeared!

If you want to read the rest of the Hannah Montana alphabet, then keep an eye out for the other books in the series!